To Toni, Harri, and Charlie

M. R.

Harri   Charlie

To all the cats in this book:

生奶水

Happy、Amber、高麗菜、王大吉、Face、阿咪、露姬、花花、吳妮妮、Neo、阿肥、Charcoal、廖妞妞、王咪咪、胖胖、Qtt、Chubby、王岱萌、摸摸、小Do、湯圓、白雪、Cofe、楊妮妮、小安、Amy、巴特、小胡弟、Choco、老咪咪、小咪、樂樂、蔥花、紅豆、阿蓮、Soap、Mumu、王雪飛、陳咪咪、芋粿、張小樂、Sally、罵收、Muesli、Ernie、Goofy、小乖咪、決決、咪吉、張咪咪、鳥咪、趴米、阿呆、南寶、奶油、歐歐、金金、Pussy、Tora、小葵、萌萌、小金鋼、咪嚕、卡栗、khaki、貓咪、瞎瞎、髒髒、乖乖、阿蒲、阿笨、Pandalin、綠油精、喇咪、芭樂、Klavier、Two、O₂、Maoma、呂小皮、小不黑占、豆子、三三、花花、雷弟、光復路、忌廉、ttt、荳荳、小叮、捲頭、該該、Miken、小豆姜、柚子、Momo、張有為、毛弟、莊毛毛、Fubo、龍龍、黑嚕

C. L.

The Pawed Piper

Michelle Robinson   illustrated by Chinlun Lee

CANDLEWICK PRESS

I wanted a cat to cuddle.

A great big furry fluff ball,
like the cat in my book.

So I laid a trail.

Balls of wool, ribbon . . .

bowls of milk . . .

tiny balls
that jingled . . .

and soft cushions.

Now, what *else*
do cats like?

I went to see my granny.

She said that
Hector likes catnip,

cardboard boxes,

and helping to read
the newspaper.

I borrowed some things.

Then I waited. . . .

But no cats came.

Not even a kitten.

So I took my book to bed
and hugged that instead.

Then something
woke me up.

Something purry,

something furry,

something warm

and soft

and cuddly.

"Hello, Hector!

Oh, you brought a friend.
And another . . . and another!

ALL
THE
CATS!"

Five, six, seven, eight,
nine, ten, eleven . . .
I lost count at
SIXTY-SEVEN!

Fat ones, skinny ones,
massive ones, and mini ones.
Cats with spots and cats with stripes.
Grumpy cats with scowling faces,
playful ones that chased my laces.

All day long,
just me and my cats, cuddling.
It was wonderful.

I loved them all.
Especially the cat who made herself
at home in my sock drawer
and wouldn't come out.

But when I went to take
Hector home . . .

"Oh, no!"

I didn't mean to take
anyone else's cat.
I just wanted one
of my own.

Granny said I had to give them back.

ALL THE CATS.

It wasn't fair—everyone else had a cat to cuddle.

Me? I just had my book.

Although . . .

I'd forgotten about the cat in my sock drawer.

She'd been so quiet.

And now I knew why. . . .

ALL THE KITTENS!

Black ones, cream ones,

somewhere-in-between ones.

Each with tiny padded paws

and perfect elfin ears.

I loved them *all*,
and I looked after them
until it was time for them
to go to their new homes.

All except the smallest one,
who had made himself
at home in the corner
and wouldn't leave . . .

not ever.